LAKEWOOD LIBRARY/MEDIA CENTER

Z0041079   E M
Annie, Bea, and Chi Chi
                       14.99

W9-ANE-977

DATE DUE

Lakewood Library/Media Center
Holland, Mi 49424

Z41079   ; 6/96

Annie, Bea, and Chi Chi Dolores

A SCHOOL DAY ALPHABET

Lakewood Library/Media Center
Holland, Mi 49424

by Donna Maurer   pictures by Denys Cazet

ORCHARD BOOKS NEW YORK

Z0041079 6/96

Text copyright © 1993 by Donna Maurer
Illustrations copyright © 1993 by Denys Cazet
All rights reserved. No part of this book may be reproduced
or transmitted in any form or by any means, electronic or
mechanical, including photocopying, recording or by any
information storage or retrieval system, without permission in
writing from the Publisher.

Orchard Books, 95 Madison Avenue, New York, NY 10016

Manufactured in the United States of America. Printed by Barton Press, Inc.
Bound by Horowitz/Rae. Book design by Mina Greenstein.

The text of this book is set in 54 point Futura Book.
The illustrations are watercolor paintings reproduced in full color.

10 9 8 7 6 5 4 3 2 1

Library of Congress Cataloging-in-Publication Data
Maurer, Donna.
Annie, Bea, and Chi Chi Dolores : a school day alphabet /
by Donna Maurer ; pictures by Denys Cazet.   p.   cm.
"A Richard Jackson Book"—Half t.p.
Summary: Illustrations and simple text present young children
going through a day's activities at school, including counting,
follow the leader, making music, painting, and snack time.
ISBN 0-531-05467-5.   ISBN 0-531-08617-8 (lib. bdg.)
1. English language—Alphabet—Juvenile literature.
2. Schools—Juvenile literature. [1. Alphabet. 2. Schools.]
I. Cazet, Denys, ill. II. Title.
PE1155.M374 1993 92-25104

For my parents,
Sylvester and Virginia Maurer

—D.M.

A a
all aboard

B b
buddies

C c

counting

D d
drawing

E e   erasing

F f   follow the leader

G g
giggling

H h
hopping

I i
icky

J j   jumping rope

K k   kicking a ball

L l   lining up

Lakewood Library/Media Center
Holland, Mi 49424

M m   making music

N n noisy

O o

oops . . .

P p painting

Q q
quiet

R r
running races

S s   snack time

T t
tickling

U u
untangling

V v

vamoose

W w
whispering

X x
x-ing

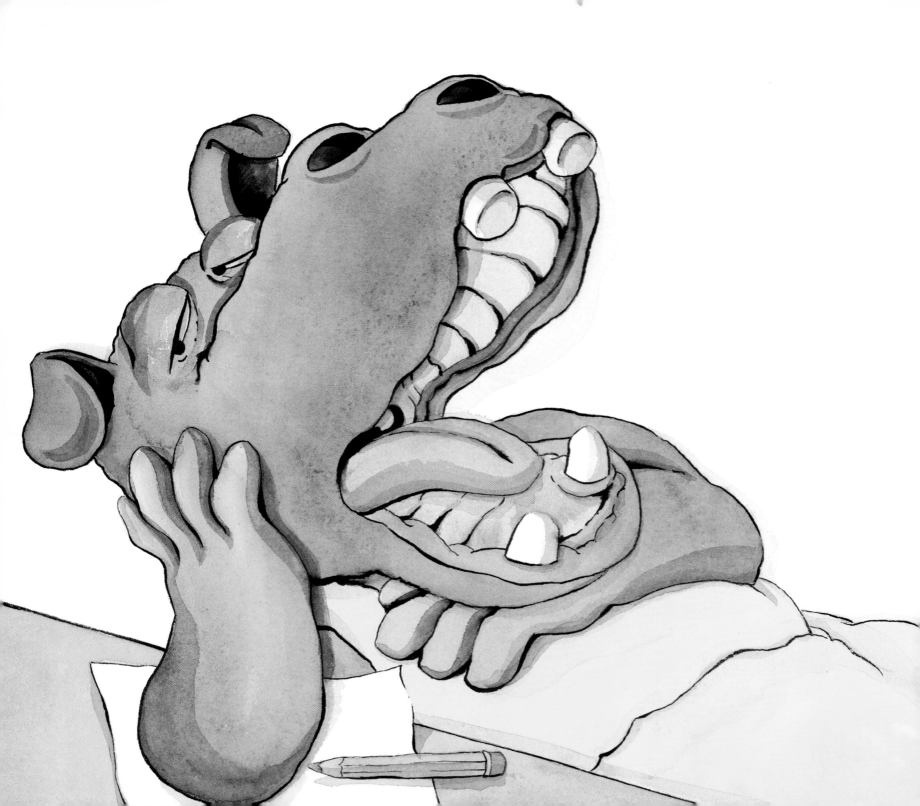

Y y   yawning

Z z

zip